Before

Rick Shepard

Contents

New Beginnings

P resent Day ...

Standing in his office, James Hamlin, a leading linguistics and history lecturer at the University, was packing up his desk. He picked up a small gilded wooden picture frame with care. The image showed a woman from behind, looking over her shoulder and smiling at the photographer. She looked happy, Hamlin smiled happily as he placed the picture into the already packed box in front of him.

'I still can't believe you're retiring,' said Amery Burton. 'You're no way older than forty five. Fifty tops!'

'A good bottle of hair colour is all you need,' said Hamlin as he chuckled softly. He ran his fingers through his hair as he smiled at Amery.

'Maybe, but you have so much left to give here.'

'It is time. I've been at this for so long and even you, my brightest student, will survive without me.'

'This uni won't,' chuckled Amery.

'It will be fine. It has managed to survive thousands of students, building closures and relocations happily enough. It will be here long after I'm gone.

'Besides, I have beaches and cocktails to look forward to.'

A knock on the door startled the both of them. Through the door came the dean. 'James, are you sure I can't convince you to stay on one more semester?'

'When the new guy gets here next week, all will be well. I've known him for five years and he will be amazing,' said Hamlin.

'Yeah, but do you need to also take Amery with you?' said the dean.

Hamlin looked curiously at Amery. Amery just looked sheepish.

'I'm leaving also, James,' said Amery. 'I have a job offer in Rome.'

'Interesting. Wow, I didn't know. Congratulations. You'll have to let me know when you're settled and I'll come visit,' said Hamlin. 'Anyway, time to get out of here. My flight is in a few hours and I still need to pack a suitcase. I have two weeks on the Costa Blanca and then a cruise around the Med for a month. And then I am going to write my memoir.'

'Can I have a signed copy?' said Amery.

The dean and Hamlin both smiled.

Hamlin walked around the desk and gave Amery a hug. He slapped the dean on the shoulder with a friendly pat, and then they shook hands. Finally, he turned and picked up his box of things. 'See you around,' he said.

He then set off from his office, from the faculty building and eventually left the campus. He didn't go and collect his car from the car park. He didn't take the chance to have one last look at the place he'd worked at for the last twenty four and a half years. He just left.

As Hamlin passed a nearby café, he stopped a moment and looked about. It was mid-afternoon on a dull, dreary Friday in the quiet period right in-between lunch and evening rush hour. Spring was ending and Summer was around the corner, but the dull weather kept people off the streets.

Down the side of the café was a large black, industrial waste bin. Hamlin stepped over to it raised the lid and dropped his box of things into it. He then walked away.

'New beginnings, my love,' he said to the empty alleyway.

A moment later, after a spark of memory, he ran back to the waste bin and retrieved the photo of the woman in the gilded frame, which he then placed into an inside pocket.

Hamlin crossed the street from the café over to the nearest taxi stand, there were two black cabs waiting. He stepped up to the first one, leaned in through the window and spoke to the driver.

'Hey, here is a fifty,' and in his hand was a crisp, red fifty pound note, 'take a ride over to Piccadilly Train Station _'

'In Manchester? That's not worth all that much,' said the taxi driver as he pointed to the money.

'Yes. Where else? This fifty is yours. No questions asked. Just tell your dispatch if you need to that you are heading over to Piccadilly with a fare. And if anyone asks, tell them your passenger looked like me,' said Hamlin.

The taxi driver shrugged, took the money and said, 'Easy money.'

Hamlin then stepped up to the second black cab and climbed inside. 'Manchester Airport Departures please.'

'Sure thing, boss,' said the driver.

Across the street, Amery watched with curiosity. Amery was too far to hear what was being said, but they were good at lip reading, a lifetime of hearing issues meant they didn't need to hear what someone was saying. They could literally see the words uttered by Hamlin.

There were no more black cabs to take right then, but Amery took out their phone and called a ride share service. Hamlin would have a huge head start, but maybe, just maybe, there was enough time to catch up.

Pax Romana

2 7 BCE …

Julius Hadriana watched the sacrificial lamb being paraded along Sacred Way. From his vantage point in his villa he could see throngs of people lining the street, which made him smile. He would be joining some of them soon at the temple.

In the crowd waiting for the parade people were singing songs to Jupiter; some were swaying to the rhythm of the song, lost in thought and prayer. The rest, mainly children, ran around and played games around their parents oblivious to the importance of the day.

Today was the first ides since the founding of Romana Imperium, and it was a special one. The sacrifice to Jupiter, the King of the Gods, was held every ides, but after today Roma would be the capital of the great Roman Empire. And hearts were overflowing with love for everyone.

Well, nearly everyone. Hallus was standing behind his master, assuming the deferent position every slave should. Garallius Gabinus, Hallus' master and owner, was standing at the side of the parade waiting for the lamb to pass him by.

'Hallus! Get me into a better position. I need to touch the fleece for that will bring good omens to House Gabinus,' said Garallius.

'Yes, Dominus,' replied Hallus.

Hallus, a burley man, gently stepped around his master and then began to part the crowd before his master. 'Move it, dog. For Dominus Garallius Gabinus. He is to touch the fleece of the lamb,' shouted Hallus

The phrase 'touch the fleece' rippled through the crowd. Many were now adding the phrase to their song, some were already trying to get better positions so they, too, could 'touch the fleece'.

The centurion commanding the soldiers marshalling the crowds started to get nervous. He didn't want the crowd surging onto the street and blocking the path. He called to his optiones, his second-in-command officers of each mantiple below him, 'Any peregrinus that steps beyond the cordon are to be dispatched, by order of Emperor Augustus!'

In truth, the new emperor had issued no such edict, but the centurion thought that in saying so no one would question him.

Garallius scoffed, 'The Emperor would say no such thing! Hallus, get these peasants to part.'

Hallus forced his way through. One man, a market trader visiting Roma for the first time didn't move. Hallus punched him once on the chin with such force that the man collapsed in a heap. No one but Hallus, Garallius and the market trader witnessed the incident, but it was enough to cause a distraction in the crowd. The crowd parted before Hallus and Garallius followed until Hallus was at the front, when they switched places and Hallus took up his usual spot behind his owner.

Julius had left his villa and was making his way to the temple citadel to Jupiter on Capitoline Hill. That was the destination for the parade, this day and all previous ides. The crowds lining the streets would soon follow the lamb when it passed them, and the soldiers would let as many as they saw fit into the temple to watch the Flaminica Dialis, the high priestess of Jupiter, sanctify not only this ides as they always did, but some saw this as the sanctification of the new Roman Empire.

At the citadel, Julius took up a position of authority as befitting a senator of Rome. Being only twenty four, Julius was young for a senator. His family name and house were strong, though, and after the death of his father Julio, he effectively inherited the position of senator.

From where he was standing he could see all who were permitted to enter. A commotion at the door from another senator Julius recognised as Garallius was catching his attention.

Behind Garallius was the ever present Hallus filling in the space between his owner and the rest of the crowd trying to gain entry.

'If you do not allow me entry, I will have you fighting in the gladiator games in the morning. As a slave!' screamed Garallius. 'I am a senator of Our glorious empire and you will treat me with all respect that position demands!'

'Centurion,' called Julius, 'allow the senator entry.'

The centurion stepped aside for a moment and bowed his head to allow Garallius to enter, but quickly stepped back in the way of anyone else. Hallus fumed, but his position was one of deference still. Julius could see the tight jaw of Hallus from where he stood. Hallus kept quiet, and Garallius did nothing for his servant.

'Centurion, close the doors,' said Garallius.

The look of hurt from Hallus to his master was clear to all.

A tinkling bell brought the attention of all within the citadel temple. The Flaminica Dialis was entering. The only sound aside from the echoes of the bell were the bleats of the lamb. Its fleece was as pure white as any ever seen before in this temple, surely a good omen for the coming celebrations.

'Celebrants,' said the Flaminica Dialis, 'welcome. Please lift up your hearts in joy to Jupiter, the King of the Sky. The highest deity in our skies.'

The high priestess then raised her arms above her head, in her hand a silver dagger glinted in the late morning sun coming through the windows.

Another bell rang and the priestess brought the dagger down in one swift movement, straight into the heart of the lamb. There was a squeal, and then silence.

'May the blessings of Jupiter rest upon all of our houses,' said the priestess.

The blood from the wound poured onto the altar, into channels running along the edges of the stone plinth. Little red rivers combined into one that met in a single pool. The blood was collected into a golden bowl. When the bowl was filled to three quarters, the priestess picked it up high above her head. 'Oh Jupiter, God of Life, accept this offering.'

The priestess returned the bowl to where she'd collected it from, a movement accompanied by another chime of the bell.

Four slave girls, all dressed in flowing white robes, each came up to the altar and filled a smaller bowl of the blood. The priestess was pouring an equal amount of blood into each of the slave girl's bowls.

The slave girls then passed amongst the celebrants in the temple and dabbed a blood stained finger into the palm of each one.

A few moments later everyone within the temple had a red print on their palm, and they were all now making their way out of the temple.

Apart from the priestess, Garallius and Julius were the last people in the temple. Julius allowed Garallius to exit before him.

'I knew your father, Julius Hadriana,' said Garallius. 'He was an inspiring man.'

'Thank you,' said Julius.

'Such a shame when he died.'

'He left a hole, that I have strived to fill.'

Garallius just nodded. Outside he spotted Hallus and shouted him over. 'Slave! Bring my parasol, this afternoon heat is unbearable.'

Hallus ran over with a silk parasol, but it wasn't quick enough for Garallius. 'You're useless.' Garallius then took a swipe at Hallus, who ducked. 'How dare you!'

Garallius took a small flail from a hidden pocket and began whipping his slave. He hit Hallus several times before Julius interjected.

'Garallius, is there any need?' said Julius.

'You would do the same to your slaves. Oh, that's right. You don't believe in keeping them,' said Garallius.

'I see no-' began Julius.

'Yes, yes. You stick to those ideals as long as they don't impact my life.' As if to make the point, Garallius swung his flail high above his head and swung down hard and fast several times onto the back of Hallus.

On the second or third swing, Garallius wasn't sure, it happened so quickly, the flail caught Julius across the face. The hardened leather strip drew blood across the left cheek of Julius.

Another senator, a rival of Garallius, saw the incident and stepped up, grabbed Garallius' hand and prevented him from swinging the flail again.

Garallius tried to brush off the incident. 'Julius, you were standing too close.'

'No,' said the man holding Garallius by the forearm. 'You can now expect retribution. Centurion! Arrest Garallius Gabinus.'

'No, I-' began Garallius.

Julius was holding a cloth to his face, the blood running from his wound was soaking into it.

'I can take my recompense in any way I see fit. Therefore, I will take your holdings. Centurion, release him. He is no-one of any concern. He should be escorted to his home to wrap up his affairs,' said Julius.

Garallius was about to protest, but the centurion reached for his weapon. The senator who'd stopped Garallius removed the brooch of office pinned to the shamed man's toga.

'Hallus, is it?' asked Julius of the cowering slave. Hallus just nodded. 'Come with me, let's leave the centurion to do his job.'

'Yes, Dominus,' said Hallus.

Flight

Present Day...

In the back of the cab, Hamlin reached to and caressed the scar across his left cheek as he remembered how he'd received it. That day was one he could never forget. He softly chuckled to himself as he thought back to those days.

'Something funny, boss?' said the driver.

'Just thinking of beginnings. And just about to start a new life,' said Hamlin.

From a pocket on his jacket and pulled out a small, clear plastic bag. Inside the bag was a salt-and-pepper style wig that he put on immediately. His usual light brown locks were hidden beneath the wig neatly.

The tax driver looked in his rear-view mirror as Hamlin was donning the wig and was a little confused, but never mentioned anything. When he turned around and asked for payment at the airport, he had to hide a smirk but accepted the money without another word.

Hamlin exited the black cab and headed for the departure desks. From another pocket he fished out his passport and a ticket in a red and white envelope; this had the logo of SkyLine Airways along the front.

At the check-in desks there was a queue of families heading for pre-Summer sun, with little ones in tow. Hamlin feared that this would be a painful flight with screaming kids and fed-up parents. He was thankful he had upgraded to first class and was looking forward to the extra leg room.

In the queue ahead of him were two families, one with two kids and one with just one, and an elderly couple. The elderly couple were at the front of the queue and as they were called forward there was the usual slow shuffle forward as groups had to manhandle their luggage to fill up the newly free space before them.

On the SkyLine desks there were three out of five possible desks open, and Hamlin was hoping they would open the others to speed things along.

At the same time that Hamlin reached the front of the queue, Amery pulled up to the airport in the ride share car they had arranged. Standing in the entrance way to Departures, Amery looked about, trying to spot Hamlin.

In front of Amery were the SkyLine desks and they could see there was a man of Halmlin's build at the front waiting to be served. The issue was, however, that the man had black and grey hair, and Hamlin had brown hair.

Hamlin was casually looking about when he saw that Amery had just entered the building. For a brief second, they locked eyes and Hamlin froze. Thankfully, he heard the man behind the check-in desk call, 'Next please!'

Without having to try and hide his reaction to seeing Amery, he quickly turned to the desk to begin the check-in process.

'Welcome to Manchester Airport, Mister Stafford,' said the airline rep behind the desk. He was oblivious to anything other than the passport and the ticket. 'Do you have any luggage to check in?'

'No. I already checked my bags in with an overnight check-in yesterday,' said Hamlin.

'Perfect. Well, that is all in order, sir. You have a good flight,' the rep said distractedly as he handed back the ticket and passport.

Hamlin wondered how many times these reps must say that and actually mean it, but then paid no mind to it and headed away from the check in desks.

Without turning his head, he decided to walk with a slight limp, but he walked briskly to the stairs for the departure lounges. From the corner of his eyes, he could see Amery following his movements. He was desperately trying to remain casual and not draw attention to himself.

Amery was watching this older version of Hamlin walk along to the stairs. The man had similar clothing to those they last saw Hamlin wearing, and aside from the hair and the limp, this was Hamlin.

'Prof!' called Amery. 'Wait a minute,' they said.

Hamlin tried hard not to react, but he turned his head slightly. Amery took that as proof they were right and began to quickly walk over to intercept.

'Hello?' said Hamlin as Amery stepped in front of him. He had added a northern accent to his speech to hide behind.

Amery was confused for a moment by the accent, but continued. 'Thought you were going to Spain, not,' Amery paused whilst they tried to sneak a peak at the ticket in Hamlin's hand, 'not Paris.'

'I am not sure my travels are your concern,' said Hamlin. 'Have we met before?'

'Don't hide behind that false accent. And is that a wig? What's going on here?' Amery was getting louder and louder as they spoke.

Hamlin looked furious for a moment, then he took Amery by the elbow and led them off to one side, away from the passing crowds. 'Keep your voice down,' he hissed in his normal voice.

'I knew it!' Amery replied.

'Please!' Hamlin sighed. He pinched the bridge of his nose and scrunched his eyes. 'Yes, it is me. Very clever. Why are you following me?'

'I saw you dumping your things before you then tried a fakeroo with two black cabs. But I can lip read. I thought you were going home to pack, but instead you came straight here. No suitcases, and just a mysterious item you fished out of that bin.' Amery then looked at the slight bulge on Hamlin's jacket where the picture frame was stored in an inside pocket.

Hamlin instinctively reached for the picture and sighed again.

'Listen, I need to catch my flight,' said Hamlin. 'Things change Amery, things move on. I can't do this life any-more and I need to change. I wish you all the best but I need to go.'

'I guess you won't be coming to see me in Rome,' said Amery.

'I am not trying to hurt you, or anyone,' said Hamlin as he started up the stairs. 'Genuinely I wish you a great future. I've seen you grow, and grow, and I know you will be amazing at whatever you do. Take care.'

Hamlin then waved at Amery with his the hand hold-ing his ticket. He was smiling with affection as he then stepped out of sight at the top of the stairs. Amery was standing at the bottom of the stairs with a small tear running down their cheek.

Spring in Paris

Hamlin was being shaken awake by one of the cabin crew. 'Sir, we've landed. Time to disembark,' said the man in French.

Throughout the flight, whenever spoken to Hamlin had spoken in French, or with a subtle French accent, to the crew and his fellow passengers. He was intent on showing a completely different personality to what anyone who knows him would recognise. That way, when anyone was asked, as he had seen many times before, they would not be able to make the connection to him and his new life.

As he stepped through the exit way of the plane, about to descend the stairs to the waiting bus, he paused and took a deep breath. It was just after noon when the flight landed at Charles de Gaul airport and the crisp spring air felt great. It certainly helped him to wake up and throw off the last vestiges of sleep.

When he boarded the bus his thoughts turned to the last time he was in Paris for any length of time.

---✯=✯---

1889CE...

'Hallus, my old friend, I love Paris at this time of year. These crowds however are too much,' said the tall man in a white suit and top hat.

'Don't call me Hallus, please Dominus,' replied Hall. 'I go by Hall Libertini these days.'

'Dominus? Really? Aren't we beyond that by now?' the tall man smiled making the scar along his cheek crease as he did. 'I like your new name, shows your true self while remaining simple. But please, you really must stop calling me Dominus. I gave you your freedom from the very start.'

'I remember. Our pact was my way of showing my gratitude,' replied Hall.

The tall man continued, 'And I have been grateful for that ever since. Please call me James, that is the name I use these days. I dropped Julius a long time ago and I often change my surname. Currently I'm using Sanderson, but after spending time recently in Germany I'm inspired to change to Hamelin.'

'After the piper story?' said Hall

'Exactly. It is a few hundred years old, but in the last few years I have been taking on various teaching positions, with a focus on literature. The story just struck a chord with me from the first time I heard it.'

'James Hamelin? Has a ring to it,' smiled Hall. 'Oh, and it is more than a story. One day I will tell you more.'

The tall man smiled again at his friend. 'Are we going to see this tower Monsieur Eiffel has built? We have come a long way to see this feat of modern engineering.'

'After you, Dominus,' said Hall.

The other man looked curiously at Hall.

'Sorry, old habits are hard to break,' said Hall.

The two men proceeded towards the newly opened Eiffel Tower to join the throngs already gathering for the opening ceremony.

'How long has it been since we last met?' asked the tall man.

'Probably over a hundred years,' said Hall. 'Do you ever tire of this life?'

'Not once.'

---★=★---

Present Day...

The bus pulled up to the terminal building and everyone disembarked. Hamlin held back, allowing all the others to get off first. He had to pull off another quick change, but he didn't want any witnesses.

As soon as Hamlin saw a rest room, he ducked inside, checked there were no other occupants, and then removed his wig. He stuffed the wig into the little plastic bag again and retrieved a pair of black rimmed glasses.

From another pocket he pulled out three passports. He opened the blue coloured one and checked the name, James Henry Stamford. He'd started using a middle name around the start of the twentieth century because he thought it made him sound distinguished.

At passport control he gave over the Stamford passport.

'Welcome to Paris Monsieur Stamford,' said the officer checking his passport as he handed it back. Hamlin smiled and then passed through to claim his luggage.

He had indeed checked in luggage the night before his flight. It was a small case with few belongings within; mostly clothing and shoes, just enough to get him through a night or two at some hotel.

Passing through the departure area he saw a copy of today's edition of Le Monde. The headline caught his eye:

DOUBLE MEURTRE AU RITZ

'A murder at the Ritz?' thought Hamlin. Hairs raised up on his neck. Death is something that you get used to with a long life, but this one, these two, had something about them that was cause for concern.

Hamlin had a suite booked at The Ritz for the next three days. He was then scheduled to meet Hall again for the first time in many years. These deaths were unusual in such a high class location, and there were friends, no family, of his staying there waiting to see him.

Eloise Desrosiers, and her son, were waiting for him. From what Hamlin could recall and work out, Eloise would be ninety in a few days, just before Hamlin was due to leave for Vienna. Her son Benard, was approaching seventy.

Eloise and Hamlin were married once upon a time. It felt like many lifetimes ago now, but he longed to see her long blonde hair and deep blue eyes once more.

Hamlin raced to the taxi rank, barked adestination for the hotel and prayed to Jupiter that Eloise was unhurt.

Heartbreak Hotel

When Amery arrived home, emotions were running strong. Having gone through various states from crying to anger, and back to crying. The driver of the ride-share they were in asked many times if they needed any help. Each time Amery declined, and insisted on just getting home.

But there appeared to be no safe harbour there either.

The front door to Amery's flat had been forced, the lock was hanging loose. Shaking with fear, Amery gently pushed the door inwards with their fingertips.

'Hello?' Amery called.

There was no response.

Amery pulled out a mobile phone and started to dial for the police. It was clear the intruder was no longer in Amery's home, so they called the non-emergency number.

The call was answered within a few rings by a bored sounding woman. 'Police, how can I help?'

'My flat has been broken into. I'm standing at the door and someone has booted the door in. I've not gone in, I'm too scared.' Amery said. They tried to keep their voice calm and even, but they couldn't hide a slight quiver as they spoke.

'OK, can you give me your address?' replied the woman.

Amery rattled off their address.

'Sorry, can you repeat that. Just a little slower.'

Amery cleared their throat and slowly repeated the address.

'Thank you. Is the intruder still in your home?'

'No. I don't think so. I can't hear any noise from inside,' Amery said.

'Perfect. Is there some where you can go for now? Until we can send someone round?' said the woman.

'Possibly. How long will it be before someone can come round?'

'Given the fact the intruder is no longer there, the urgency is low,' said the operator, 'and that means we have time to send the right team round. Would need to ask your landlord to secure the flat until then. Is that something you can do?'

'I will speak to them next,' Amery said.

The operator gave Amery a crime number and wished them well before ending the call.

---✮=✮---

Amery was still shaking when they were knocking on the office door of the building manager. It was just after two in the afternoon, meaning that the office should have someone in there. Usually, the building management team were on-site between ten in the morning to three in the afternoon. At least one person.

A moment later a smartly dressed man opened the door. His janitorial styled uniform looked crisp and clean. Amery thought that this man had done nothing harder than making a cup of tea all day.

'My flat has been broken into,' Amery told the man.

'Oh? Which unit?' he said.

'Mine is thirty one.' Amery then showed their phone with an image of the busted front door.

'We can't have that,' he said, brightly. He then went to collect his tool box. 'I assume you've called the police. Leave it with me now. I'll secure your property until the crime team turn up.'

Amery nodded. 'You'll let me know when they arrive?'

'Of course. We've got your details on the system so I'll go up there now and block the doorway up until the police arrive. Don't want opportunists to cause more harm. I've seen this take a couple of hours before, so you get off. Go spend time with family and friends. Get them to make you a sugary cup of tea. Try not to worry.'

Despite their initial assessment, this janitor appeared to genuinely care and that helped Amery relax a little. Yes, this was a stressful situation, but there was now light at the end of this scary tunnel.

---★=★---

Amery called their Mum. She lived outside the city of Manchester in nearby Stalybridge. Just a short bus ride away. 'Mum, my flat been broken into.'

'Oh, sweetheart. No. That's awful,' Amery's mother said. 'Are you ok?'

'I'm fine,' Amery said, 'I was at college. My last day there, I was saying my goodbyes.'

'Goodness. You need to come home.' Amery's mother always said that 'home' was wherever love was.

'Thanks, Mum.' Amery then broke down in tears again.

---★=★---

In Paris, the taxi carrying Hamlin pulled up to the front of the Ritz. A doorman opened the door and Hamlin stepped out.

'Bonjour, Monsieur. Bienvenue à Paris.' The doorman then asked to take Hamlin's bags and led the way into the foyer.

Inside the Ritz were a number of Gendarmerie officers. They were standing guard at strategic points around the area; casually trying to blend in and be part of the furniture and fixtures.

One officer was standing next to the lifts, his hand casually resting next to his sidearm and staring intensely at Hamlin. It made Hamlin feel uncomfortable for a moment before he shrugged it off and headed for the reception desk. The gendarme watching Hamlin didn't take his eyes off Hamlin.

'Bonjour Monsieur,' said the smiling woman behind the desk.

It was a fake smile, Hamlin had seen it so many times before, but he didn't let that affect how he replied. 'Hi, I have a reservation for James Stafford.' He than gave over the Stafford passport.

'Of course, Monsieur Stafford,' she said. Her accent was soft and lilting. She then began typing on her keyboard. 'Ah, oui. We have you in the Suite Chopin for three nights. Here is your key card. There is also a message for you. Another guest, from our- '

She stopped mid-sentence. A look of horror passed briefly over her face, she wasn't quick enough to hide the expression from Hamlin.

He read her name tag. 'Camille, what's the message?'

Camille looked over to the gendarmes, and then to her supervisor. 'Andre, Monsieur Stafford est ici et nous avons le message de Suite Imperiale.' Hamlin understood every word, but pretended he didn't and shook his head with a puzzled look.

'Monsieur Stafford,' said Andre as he walked over. His name badge marked him out as a duty manager. 'There has been an incident, but there was a guest in the Suite Imperiale-'

'Was?'

'I am very sorry, I cannot say more. However, the inspector will want to have a word,' said the manager. He then motioned over to a woman in a blue business suit. 'Inspector Delisle will be able to talk to you about this.'

'Inspector, this is Monsieur Stafford. He is the recipient of the message you've been looking at.'

'Monsieur,' said Delisle, 'maybe you could help us to understand this note.'

The inspector then handed over a small, clear bag with a note inside. The handwriting was one Hamlin recognised immediately. It was written in English.

My dearest Papa J,

I fear that this may be my time to meet Jupiter. I heard about Freyja and the report disturbs me. It does not sound like an accident. Not after I read the news on the event.

Stay safe. Time for a new life once again I feel.

See you in the next one,

E

Hamlin's face went white.

The Pact

2 7 BCE... 12th of Aprilius 'Hallus,' said Julius, 'I've heard disturbing news that Garallius is plotting against you. Looking for revenge, I believe. If you are to stay safe, you need to stay away from public locations.'

'Yes, Dominus,' replied Hallus.

'Please stop calling me that. You've been granted your freedom for more than a month now. You are no longer a slave. Your antics at the market did not go unnoticed.'

'Besides the fact that those children were starving, I didn't steal.'

'There were witnesses.'

'They were friends of my previous master, I think you'll find. Loyalty buys a lot.'

'True.'

---✫=✫---

Present Day... Sitting in the foyer of the hotel, waiting for Inspector Delisle to finish her phone call, Hamlin tried to picture his daughter, Freyja, and what had happened to her. What had Eloise meant in her mail.

Hamlin had not thought of Freyja for nearly thirty years. The last time he saw her was in Cairo and they were heading in separate directions. James was heading to England, a new life as a lecturer at Manchester University beckoned. Freyja, then in her forties but looked much younger, had just married and was leaving for Austria with her new husband.

Freyja had known that her father was ageless, and she was well aware that she would never see him again after the wedding. Hamlin could see, however, that she would be fine. Her husband was a good man; Hamlin had made sure his future son in law had no skeletons in his past that would cause his daughter any issues. He never expected to be reading about her murder.

With his phone in his hand he'd searched up for the news that Eloise had mentioned. It was a disturbing article, and Hamlin thought it sounded a little ritualistic.

'Monsieur Stafford, apologies. That was my superiors. There has not been a murder in this hotel in many years, if ever. This could have an impact on not just the hotel, but Paris as a whole. How do you know the deceased, a Madamoiselle Desrosiers?' said the inspector.

'She is, sorry was, my aunt. My father's sister.' Hamlin tried to hold back tears, but one role slowly down his cheek. 'What has happened?'

The inspector took a breath, and then she sat down next to Hamlin. 'I can't go into details. It wouldn't be fair, to you, even if I did. Your aunt has been murdered I am afraid. Her and her son Benard.'

'Benard too?'

Hamlin swallowed, hard. Eloise was not his aunt, of course, she was his wife. Benard was their son.

'I'm sorry, yes. Were you close to your aunt and your cousin?'

'I'd not seen them both for a few years. We were meant to be catching up over the next week or so before I move to the US,' said Hamlin.

'You and your cousin are about the same age, yes?'

'Benard is-' Hamlin choked. 'Sorry, I can't do this. What happened to them?'

'You don't need to think about that right now. Let me get my colleagues from family support to talk to you about what happens now.'

The inspector motioned over to a couple of people loitering in the middle of the foyer area.

Hamlin still held the note from Eloise. He flipped it over a few times, half expecting more words to magically appear, but knowing that they wouldn't. After the third or fourth flip over, he spotted a symbol in the top right on the reverse of the note. It was a stylised combination of the number 2 and 4.

This was the ancient symbol for Jupiter and something Hamlin had not seen in many years. The memory of a tattoo on his shoulder blade. Another memory of its twin on a friend from many years ago.

---★=★---

27 BCE... 14th of Aprilius 'Hallus, I heard from the senate this morning that Garallius has bribed a centurion. The claim is that you've absconded from his house, and you are to be apprehended. Or executed.'

'Executed?' said Hallus.

'I have a plan to get you to Jupiter's pillar. Where a boat will be waiting for you. A man I can trust from Persia, a trader I have worked with many times, will transport you to safer shores.'

'Where is Persia?'

'It is beyond the reaches of Rome. That is really all that matters. You are my friend.'

---★=★---

Present Day... Hamlin sat in stunned silence and the family support officers were speaking, but he wasn't hearing.

In his head he just pictured the many monuments to the god Jupiter. He'd visited them all. One in particular popped into his head. Many of the monuments are in Germany, one or two he'd helped reconstruct from pieces found in excavations. The one he thought about now was in, 'Mainz.'

'I beg your pardon, Monsieur,' said the officer.

The death of Freyja occurred in Mainz.

'I'm sorry. This note mentions Freyja and something not being an accident. I know someone named Freyja Huber.' Hamlin offered up the note. 'The reports in multiple media say Freyja was the victim of an accident. The pictures here show it is not.'

The officers were confused.

Hamlin flipped over the note and pointed at the Jupiter icon. 'This means Jupiter. Freyja was killed near the Jupiter monument in Mainz.'

'How is this Freyja linked to the events here?'

'Only me, that I know of right now. Someone is targeting my family. My friends. I have written a paper on this particular monument. Are there any symbolic references to Jupiter in the murder of my aunt?'

The officers both looked uncomfortable for a moment. One of them cleared their throat before speaking, 'Monsieur Stafford, there was this.'

The officer showed Hamlin a phone screen with an image of a a wall. On the wall, daubed in black, was the same symbol on the note Hamlin held.

---✶=✶---

27 BCE ... 6th of Maius 'It has been almost a month since we set out on this journey, Dominus.'

'It has, but we near our destination. See, the coast, that is Mons Calpe,' pointed Julius.

'I can see the port, but I think we need to wait here a moment. You have saved my life, more than once. And I need to repay you.' Hallus then took out a small blade and cut across his left palm.

Julius looked on with horror.

'Please, Dominus, don't be concerned,' said Hallus. He handed the knife, hilt first, to Julius.

Julius took the knife.

'This will be a good thing, I promise. If you make this oath with me, only good things can happen.'

Reluctantly, Julius placed the blade against his palm and cut in the same way. Palms dripping with blood they clasped hands. A strong grip from both.

'As you have saved my life, I will save yours. Forever. As long as I live, so will you. Under the eyes of Jupiter, at the sight of Mons Calpe, you will live forever.' Hallus gripped harder on the hand of his friend.

'No one lives forever,' said Julius.

Hallus smiled brighter. 'Do you know what they call Mons Calpe?'

Julius shook his head.

'This is a pillar of Jupiter. There are others, but this is the tallest. Jupiter has looked over us both from that first day when Caesar Augustus closed the Gates of Janus, through to today. And he will beyond. We must part now. Tell me the name of your friend, I will find him.'

'Azar. He will be the most flamboyant person around. Always with a flourish,' replied Julius.

'Go, my friend. We will meet again. You must go and return to your family.'

Family

P resent Day... Amery went home. Their mother laid on all their old favourites; Sunday roast, even though it was not a Sunday, a slushy romance movie, all washed down with a bottle of fine red wine.

'Mum, this is just the day the I needed. Thank you,' said Amery.

'For you, any time. You're my world. What has happened is awful,' she gave Amery a big hug.

Amery returned the hug. 'I need to go to Paris. There's someone I need to find.'

'But I thought your job was in Rome.'

'That's not for another month. My friend rushed off to Paris, and I think he's in trouble.' Amery looked down at their hands. 'He quit his job, and moved away without taking his belongings. Looks like he's trying to hide from something.'

'Is he in danger?'

'Not sure,' Amery shrugged, but then quickly continued when they saw the expression on their mother's face. 'I don't think so. It's probably financially motivated. He's never had much. Not that I've seen, anyway.'

'Okay. So when are you going?'

'I have my passport, I was thinking of going on the first flight tomorrow. I've already booked a cheap hotel near the centre of Paris,' said Amery.

'Does your friend know you're going?'

'He doesn't, but I know he always stays at the Ritz. He talks about that place as though he saw it being built. Money worries or not, I reckon he's a real creature of habit. So even if it's one last time, I bet he's there right now.' Amery then drained their glass and stood.

'You'll be careful, won't you? Don't go getting into anything dodgy.' Amery's mother had a stern expression.

'Mum! I'm not an idiot,' Amery replied.

---★=★---

In his hotel room Hamlin sat and stared at the wall. Yesterday had been more than difficult. He could barely get any sleep with thoughts of what was going on running through his head constantly.

He'd woken this morning, dressed and then sat down. His breakfast was hardly touched. Inside he was numb.

His wife, his son and his daughter had all been killed. And he couldn't tell anyone about it. He had to lie. Not to protect himself, but to protect the memory of those that died.

If there was any suspicion about how old Eloise or Benard really were, or who they really were to him, there'd be far too many awkward questions to answer.

Living as long as he had, he was used to loved ones passing into the care of Jupiter, but this was different.

There were scant details released by the French police, so he could only guess what happened to Eloise. However, the German media had picked up the story about Freyja and the reports didn't make for pleasant reading.

A knock at his door startled him.

'Who is it?'

'Monsieur Stafford it is the hotel manager. Can we speak?'

Hamlin stood and opened the door. A man shorter than he stood in the hallway, there was a badge on his lapel that identified him as Antoine and below his name was the word Directeur. Hamlin stood aside and motioned for the man to enter.

'Merci, Monsieur.' The man walked into the centre of the room.

'Please, take a seat,' said Hamlin.

'This won't take a moment,' replied Antoine. 'In light of recent events, and in respect to your Aunt. We'd like to reimburse your stay and let you know you can stay for a long as needed. I believe that the police would like to speak with you again this morning.

'Yes, the inspector has asked that I go to her office later to look at some photos I believe.

'Very good, sir.' Antoine then headed for the door. 'Oh, pardon, I forgot. There is a young person waiting for you in the foyer. They were insistent on seeing you.

Antoine let the door close on the confused Hamlin

---✫=✫---

Hamlin exited the lift and stared around the foyer area, looking for anyone familiar. A shock of blue hair caught his attention.

'Amery, what are you doing here?' he said as he approached.

Amery turned and smiled. 'I know. It's a shock, but here I am.

'How- ' began Hamlin.

'You've talked this place up many times, Professor. It's like you saw the first brick being laid in place. So I took a while stab, and struck gold. Obviously.

'What's with all the police?' Amery finished.

'There's been an incident and the hotel is under their protection at the moment. Why are you here?

'I got the idea that you're in trouble. These police are connected to you somehow aren't they?' Amery looked at Hamlin with a concerned expression.

'Yes. No. Not exactly. It's not safe you being here,' he said.

'My flat was broken into and done over. Police are here because of you. These are not normal times.'

'Your flat? Are you ok?' It was Hamlin's turn to be concerned.

'I'm fine. I stayed at my Mum's. The police have nothing yet, but they promised to get back to me when they do. The janitor in my building has made the flat secure.'

Thoughts of Amery's mother sprang into Hamlin's memory. 'Is your mother OK?'

A look of a question crossed Amery's face briefly. 'She's fine.

'Listen, it's good to see you, but I have an appointment with the police inspector.'

'Come on then, let's go,' Amery said grabbing their coat.

Hamlin sighed. He knew he wouldn't be able to do this without Amery tagging along anyway, so he just nodded.

The short ride to the police station was completed in silence. The gendarme driving didn't speak much English and neither Hamlin nor Amery felt like talking.

At the station Inspector Delisle met them both. 'Who is this?' the inspect asked Hamlin.

'This is Amery, my friend from the UK. They are stopping over here on their way to a new job in Rome.'

Delisle just nodded and shook Amery's hand.

'Monsieur Stafford, my condolences again. I know this is difficult, but if you could look through these folders to see if you recognise anyone that could be a big help in our investigations.'

Amery stayed silent until the inspector left the room. 'Stafford? Condolences? What's really going on here,' they said.

Hamlin ignored the questions and began to open the first of three black folders.

Inside the folder was photos. Hundreds of them. The many pages within were making this first folder bulge more than the covers should reasonably hold. A thought struck Amery on why they were using physical photos rather than digital on a tablet or a computer screen instead, but they left their thoughts unspoken.

Many of the photos in this first book were mug-shot style head-and-shoulders. There were also pages of stills taken from CCTV cameras, some were grainy and indecipherable but many had been enhanced to try and reduce the blurry photo. It was obvious they'd been touched up.

Amery looked over Hamlin's shoulder as he flipped page after page. By the time Hamlin opened the next book, they were both hardly looking at the images by this point, the photos were starting to blur into one, and Hamlin was flipping the pages quickly.

In the second folder, one image caught Amery's attention.

'Whoa, slow down there,' Amery said. 'Go back a page. No another. There!'

'What is it?' Hamlin said.

'That man. Him there,' Amery stabbed a finger at a mug-shot of a long haired man. 'He was coming out of my building when I got home to find my flat was burgled.'

Hamlin knew Amery had a photographic memory and didn't question what they were saying. He looked hard at the photo a moment and then gasped. 'Hallus.'

Revelations

'Who?' Amery said.

It was one word that Hamlin was expecting, but one he really didn't want to answer. Nor could he see a sensible way to answer without sounding crazy. He knew he'd have to tell Amery the truth, he just didn't know how they would react.

'Hallus is someone I knew a very long time ago. We parted ways so long ago, and I've not seen him since.' Hamlin chuckled quietly.

'Who is he?'

'He's the reason for many things. Some of those are too true to believe, but true they are.

'We met in Rome. How can I say this?' Hamlin paused for a moment. 'He was, working for a rival who attacked me in public. The authorities were involved, things were said, he came to work for me, then Hallus and I became partners. We parted friends after each meeting. At least I thought so.'

Amery looked at Hamlin with concern. 'You're thinking otherwise now?'

Hamlin scoffed. 'I don't know what to think. I really want to know how he has linked you and I together-'

'You and I? What does that mean? You think he came after me because of you, don't you?' Amery's voice was getting higher with each syllable. 'You need to tell me really what is going on and who you really are. Professor Hamlin. Or Monsieur Stafford. You're hiding something, and no matter what you say next, I'm involved. Spill!'

Hamlin spotted Inspector Delisle walking over. 'Not here,' he hissed.

'Monsieur Stafford, any progress?' said the inspector.

'Yes. My friend Amery says their flat, back in England, was broken into recently. And on their way into the building, this man,' Hamlin prodded the picture of Hallus, 'was coming out.'

'That is some coincidence,' nodded the inspector.

'Inspector?' said Hamlin.

'It's early in the investigation, but this man had been seen multiple times in the vicinity of The Ritz in the last two days.' Amery and Hamlin looked at each other.

'Well, thanks for your help so far. If we hear anything more, we'll be in touch. We've got your details Monsieur Stafford.' Delisle held out her hand to shake Hamlin's.

Hamlin shook hands with the inspector and Amery held out a hand too. The inspector obliged, along with a friendly smile.

---✦=✦---

Hamlin led Amery quickly over to a bistro across from the police station. He took a seat at a table outside, the furthest one away from the door of the establishment. Amery sat opposite. Hamlin wanted to make this look as casual as possible. It helped that the afternoon sun was still shining and a gentle warm breeze was blowing.

' Go on then,' said Amery. Impatience was clear in the tone they used.

Before Hamlin could say anything in reply, a young lad came over with a tablet in his hand. He was wearing a white shirt, black trousers and a dark brown apron with the words "La Papillon", the name of the bistro, written in a cursive font.

'Deux cafés, s'il vous plaît,' said Hamlin without missing a beat before the waiter could speak.

The young man nodded and went back inside the bistro.

Hamlin sighed, rubbed his eyes and then looked at Amery. 'Do you know how old I am?'

Amery looked confused. 'You're in your forties, right? No older than fifty, surely.'

'No.' Hamlin smiled. 'I was born so long ago that even I forget sometimes exactly when. I recall the founding of the Roman Empire, the signing of the great "Pax Romana". I've witnessed more successes and disasters than anyone ever should.'

'You're telling me you are over two thousand years old?' Amery's laugh was awkwardly cut short at the arrival of the waiter with the coffees.

'Merci,' said Hamlin. He held out a twenty Euro note, which the waiter took with a smile.

'Yes. I've always loved Paris, you know.' Hamlin's voice had shifted to wistful tone. 'I've seen too many bad and dark days here. The French Revolution was scary, I'll tell you. I had to hide or be caught, and likely beheaded, by the revolutionaries. I fought the Nazis in World War Two, to protect this city and this great nation. And free Europe from tyranny. I've seen better days too, such as the opening of the Eiffel Tower, or helping my good friend César Ritz get the money together to buy the old Hôtel de Gramon so he could create The Ritz Hotel.

'And no, I can't prove any of this. But it is all true. I've stayed in the shadows in all the events I have had a hand in. I've had to, for my own protection. For the protection of my family too.'

'How-' Amery started.

Hamlin didn't stop. 'Hallus was a slave to an unscrupu-
lous rival of mine, Senator Garallius Gabinus. There was
an incident that brought shame onto his house, as he
attacked mine. The punishment was that all of my rival's
chattels became mine. I set Hallus free, I didn't believe
in slavery. Never have, never will.

'In payment, Hallus made a pact with me that for as
long as he lived, so would I. That was in 27BC.'

Amery sat and sipped at their coffee, not saying a
word.

'The last time I saw Hallus was in Gibraltar. One of our
many trips there. Do you know what the Romans called
The Rock, originally?' Hamlin paused.

Amery stayed silent. They raised an eyebrow at the
mention of Gibraltar, however.

'Mons Calpe. The Greeks called it a Pillar of Hercules. There is another, Mons Abila, across the Mediter-
ranean.'

'I'm still not sure I believe all this,' said Amery.

'It does sound far fetched. I'll admit. Gibraltar is a
special place for Hallus and I. That was where I set him
free, where he started his life of freedom. We've met
up many times since then, but the last time was in the
1980s. That was in Gibraltar, also. Thinking back, Hallus

didn't seem himself. He was talking about being tracked, traced somehow.'

'So every few years, you disappear and start a new life?' Amery said.

Hamlin nodded as he took a sip of coffee.

'My mum was born in Gibraltar, did I ever tell you that?' Amery tried to take control of this conversation.

'I don't think you have mentioned that before,' said Hamlin.

---✯=✯---

On the third floor of the police station, Delisle watched Hamlin and Amery finish their drinks at the bistro. 'There's something that Monsieur Stafford is not telling us, Marco. Get me everything you can on him.'

A man in a blue suit standing next to the inspector nodded, and left Delisle to her pondering and watching.

---✯=✯---

At the corner of the street, in a powder blue Renault Clio, a man sat observing them. He was holding a mic set and an audio recorder, recording the conversation between Hamlin and Amery.

The man's phone ringing brought him out of his concentration. 'Boss?'

The man listened to the caller for a moment.

'Yes, Boss. The Professor and the other one-' began the man before he had to pull the phone away from his ear. The Boss was shouting some choice words.

'Sorry. Yes, your grandchild. They're both safe, the police let them go,' he paused to listen. 'Yes, I'll keep my eyes on them.'

The call ended abruptly.

The man saw Hamlin and Amery get up to leave. They called a taxi, climbed in and set off. He started his car too and began to follow them, again.

Reunion

Gibraltar, August 1983... The sun was beating down hard on the streets and squares of Gibraltar. Hamlin and Hallus sat at a table outside a small bar, Gibraltar's oldest by all accounts if the sign outside was to be believed, with a plate of fish and chips each.

'Do you remember this place?' said Hallus. 'We sat here with the good Captain Columbus.'

'I remember,' replied Hamlin.

'Those were the days.'

'Those were the days you were drunk all the time. I swear by Jupiter you were trying to end yourself at the bottom of a keg of rum.' Hamlin smiled.

'Drunk? How dare you sir,' Hallus laughed.

Hamlin joined in the laughter.

It was true, the days with Columbus were dark days for both of them. Hallus was affected hardest by their longevity it seemed and it took Hamlin months of watching his friend to keep him safe. To keep him from harming himself. Hamlin thought his friend was constantly trying to take his life.

'The free booze on tap didn't help my mood, I'll admit. But that was then.' Hallus took a large bite of his fish, and then continued. 'Have you seen the news about the Spanish Foreign Secretary meeting the British one, Geoffrey Howe?' Hallus asked.

'I've not kept up with the news of late.'

'The rumours are that there is going to be a treaty, or that Britain is going to hand over The Rock to Spain, or that the British are getting bullish over The Falklands and they're playing hardball.'

'Hand over Gibraltar? That's not going to happen.' Hamlin shook his head.

'Oh yes, I forgot. You're on Howe's team aren't you. Go on tell me, tell your oldest friend what's going to happen.'

Hamlin shifted in his seat. 'You know I can't divulge anything. Official Secrets act and all that. I could never do it somewhere so public anyhow.'

'So there is something going on?!' Hallus' dark rimmed eyes lit up for the first time since the two friends had met this time round.

Hamlin took a second to study his friend's face. The sunken look, dark eyes and disheveled hair put him on edge. 'Everything OK, Hallus?'

'All depends on who you speak to, doesn't it?'

---★=★---

Present Day... At the Ritz, Hamlin was packing his things into his holdall. 'I have to get to Germany. Tonight. You're welcome to use the room. I have it booked for another night.'

'No way. I don't know what's in Germany, but I'm coming too. Safety in numbers and all that,' Amery said.

'Amery. I don't know what's going on, but I want you to be safe. Back home with your mother.'

'Listen, this freak came into my home. I won't be safe until we understand what's happening. I know, what about my Mum? I'll call her, tell her to get away for a few days, she'll know what to do.'

Hamlin knew not to argue. He knew Amery would just track him down. So yeah, going together was probably the safer option.

'Okay. Call her, tell her you're going on a European rail trip with your old professor and tell her to go somewhere unexpected. Then let's go get your things.' Hamlin zipped up his bag with a flourish.

---★=★---

On an express train from Paris, Hamlin and Amery headed for Frankfurt.

'What's in Frankfurt?' Amery asked.

'My fr-' Hamlin stopped himself. 'My daughter,' he said after a pause. 'Freyja. Here,' he handed his phone to Amery.

On the phone screen was the report of the killing of Freyja and her husband.

Amery gasped at the details. 'This is awful. Is this what happened in Paris too?'

'Delisle is tight-lipped so I don't know for sure. And the French police have not connected the two, but I have,' said Hamlin.

'I'm the connection,' Hamlin turned to stare at the farmlands passing quickly by the train window. 'Freyja was my daughter, and so was Eloise. Benard was my grandson. Someone is going after my family and I need to know who and why. Then I need to stop them, by whatever means necessary.'

'We'll stop him.' Amery placed a hand on Hamlin's and smiled.

'It's about three hours before we stop, I'm going to get some food. You ok here?' Hamlin said as he stood.

Amery nodded and relaxed into the seat.

Two carriages down the train, Hamlin found a buffet bar. At the bar already was a long haired man, the hair was tied into a neat pony. It was Hallus, and he had two coffees in from of him.

Hallus smiled and gestured towards the cups. Hamlin's shoulders sagged a little before he walked over and picked up one of the cups.

'What are you doing here, Hallus?'

'Protecting my interests. As always. You're off to see what happened to Freyja, yes?' Hallus took a sip of the remaining coffee.

'Of course. But if I find out that you're-'

'I had nothing to do with that. I'm really sorry for your loss. You're my oldest friend, why would I do anything to harm that?' Hallus said.

Hamlin looked at Hallus with a sideways glance. 'I don't know what is going on. I suppose you've heard about Eloise and Benard too. This is not what should be happening.'

'I read the reports in the German media. Looks ritualistic. There's some odd iconography in the photos. You're good at this sort of thing so you need to look deeper,' Hallus nudged his friend.

'Who is Amery to you?' Hamlin asked.

Hallus looked confused.

'They spotted you, and coincidentally around the time their flat was broken into.'

'Ah,' was all Hallus could reply with.

'Amery has a photographic memory, there was no way getting around this one. We identified you at the police station in a grainy CCTV image. The police want to talk to you,' said Hamlin.

'That could be awkward. Well, I didn't do the flat. It was like that when I went looking for Amery. I wanted to make sure that they,' Hallus emphasised the word "they" as if he'd never used that term before when referring to Amery, 'were safe. Amery's mother is my daughter.'

'So you're another one!' Amery shouted. 'And what are you doing talking to this man, the one who ransacked my flat!'

'I never touched your flat,' Hallus held up his hands in surrender.

'Amery, I thought you were waiting,' said Hamlin at the same time.

'You were taking too long,' Amery said to Hamlin and then they looked to Hallus, 'And what is this about you and my Mum?'

Hallus raised his eyebrows.

'Yeah, I heard you,' said Amery, eyebrow raised and "don't mess with me look". After a couple of deep breaths and calming motions, Amery continued, 'So, you're the long lost father my mum never talks about. We don't even have any pictures of you. Come to think of it, there's not many of you either Prof.' Amery then placed a stool between the two men.

'That's a deliberate choice. Harder to do these days with the presence of all these phones, but necessary,' said Hallus.

Hamlin passed his phone to Amery again. This time there was a zoomed in image of the crime even for Freyja. 'What do you make of that?' he said.

Amery tried to zoom the image further, but couldn't. 'That's "malum", an old word for evil and that one there looks like it could be old Latin for "Immortals", but it's obscured a little. "malum vivit in corde Immortalium" I think it says. It's hard to read.'

'Evil lives in the Immortals heart,' both Hamlin and Hallus said.

'It's us,' said Hamlin. 'Whoever this is, they're coming after us. Hallus, you need to get back to England. For your daughter.'

'Oh, she's safe. She's gone camping with her mate. Unless you actually followed her, you won't find her,' said Amery.

Hamlin and Hallus both looked at her.

'I told her to go incognito, like when I told everyone I was non-binary. There was a lot of trolling when I did it and Mum faced a lot of that crap, so we came up with a plan. She and I went incognito, basically random, wild camping for a bit. We both have a grab-bag of stuff and when we've had enough of the world for a bit, we just go. She hasn't even got a phone. But she knows my number and said she will call me if, when she sees a phone box somewhere.'

'Does she drive?' asked Hallus.

'She will have taken a train. I think she wanted to try Cumbria for a bit, but I don't know for sure.' Amery shrugged.

'Fair enough,' said Hamlin.

---✦=✦---

The train sped on into the early evening. The total journey was longer than their group conversation. Having planned out what they were going to do when the train reached Frankfurt, they each settled down into their own head spaces.

Amery had fallen asleep about an hour ago, Hamlin thought that his friend was hiding how worried they really were about their mother. The description of the wild camping was a clever idea, but Hamlin was not confident.

'We're nearly there I think. Should be about thirty minutes, so when we get off, do you know how to even find your daughter?' Hamlin asked Hallus.

Hallus nodded, 'Amery said you would need to be following her to find her. Well, I have that covered,' he replied. 'I won't let anything happen to her.'

Hamlin smiled. It was good to be with his friend again.

Memories of Family

At Frankfurt Station, the trio split up again.

Hamlin and Amery set off for another platform; their connecting train to Mainz was leaving in ten minutes. It would only be a forty minute journey, but it was an additional wait that put Hamlin on edge.

Hallus gave his friend a hug and set off for the nearest taxi. He was going to get a plane back to England as soon as one was available.

Hamlin and Amery had to run when they heard the tannoy announce that their train was getting ready to depart.

'I've always loved German efficiency,' said a breathless Amery as they both boarded the train. Before the two of them could find a seat, the train lurched into motion.

'I need to find Freyja's flat when we get there. She moved here about ten years ago, just after the funeral for Georg, her husband. I've not seen either Freyja or

Georg for years, but I do get an email from Freyja every now and then. She told me that she'd retired and that she wanted to spread Georg's ashes in his hometown.'

'What did Freyja do before she retired?'

'Oh, she followed the family tradition of teaching. I believe she was a principal at a high flying academy in Austria for about twenty years. But as I said, we weren't always in touch. It's hard, when you live as long as I do, to stay in people's lives. You'll find that out for yourself, I guess. At least to some degree' Hamlin smiled.

'I don't want to live forever,' said Amery.

'Who does?' replied Hamlin.

The conversation fizzled out as the train rushed onwards.

---✯=✯---

Inspector Delisle was reading the report created by Marcus Durand, a promising detective from her team. The report was all the information he could gather on James Stafford. It was too thin.

The report had a copy of a birth certificate showing that James Julius Stafford was born in London in 1981, a credit report for an expired credit card that had never been used and a grainy photocopy of a British driving license. The last page was the passport details Hamlin had used to enter France, which was accompanied with a photo of Hamlin passing through airport security.

'Is this it?' Delisle said.

'That's all there was. Looks fake to me,' Durand said.

'It's clever. It is just enough detail to get by, but not enough to get you out of trouble if someone, like us, looks hard enough. Go and pick him up. I think we need to ask more questions.' Delisle closed the file in disgust.

'Can't Boss, he's not there. He and his friend caught a train we think, headed for Germany by all accounts,' replied Durand.

'And you didn't stop him?' Delisle was enraged. 'Where have they gone?'

Durand looked taken aback by the shouting. 'What could we hold him on? I'll get someone to find out where they went.'

'No. You find out! You! Then get onto Interpol, were going to need some international help here now. Get out!'

Durand left inspector's office and grabbed his coat. 'Franco, come on. We're off.'

Durand's partner, Franco Lambert, grabbed his jacket and followed.

---★=★---

Hallus sat in the airport lounge, getting through check-in and security was a breeze with no luggage. The plane to England was scheduled to depart in around an hour, giving him time to call his man.

'Aaron, any news?' Hallus said when the call finally connected.

'Boss, all's good here. But I hate camping,' said Aaron.

'You'll live. How's my girl?' Hallus said.

'They're fine, her and her friend. They're just over the ridge from where I am, they're setting up their tent for the night. I was going to wait until they had settled down for the night before pitching mine. '

'Describe the friend.' Hallus never gave much away.

'The friend. She's taller than me, by a hair," Aaron was five foot six, 'she is blonde, but that's from a bottle, she appears to be a similar age to your daughter. Not caught a name yet, not got near enough. Going to see if I can get closer later, see what I can hear.'

'Just keep your eyes on them. I'll be with you in the morning. My flight to Manchester will be landing around midnight your time.' Hallus ended the call and sighed.

---✯=✯---

Durand and Lambert were at the Ritz.

'You go over the crime scene again,' said Durand, 'let's see if there is anything we missed. I'm going to check Stafford's room out.'

'There's nothing new in that crime scene that forensics would not have found,' Lambert said.

'Just see what you can see. You've not been in there, so I just want your take. Anything new, odd or just different, tell me first.' Durand was keen to impress Delisle and didn't want to go back empty handed.

Whilst Lambert set off to the third floor, Durand headed for the fourth. The receptionist had given him a key to Stafford's room. Apparently he had not actually checked out, the concierge wasn't even aware he'd left the hotel.

In Stafford's room, the detective was surprised by how little the room had been used. The "do not disturb" hanger had been placed on the outside, so not even the housekeeping staff had been inside.

The bed was either unused, or Stafford, Durand surmised, had made the bed to a hospital standard.

Durand was startled by his phone ringing. 'What did you find? Anything?' he asked. 'What's with all this old Latin? And this iconography?' Lambert asked.

'Some crap about immortality? Yeah, no one has been able to decipher it. We can see what it said, and we can translate it, but what it is in connection to the murder is unknown yet.'

'Yeah, but I've seen this before, this particular face. I'm sure it was carved into a pillar or monument. And this symbol of a combined 2 and 4 is familiar also,' said Lambert.

'Where?' said Durand.

'Somewhere in Germany, I think. I was a kid, so it was a while ago.'

---✫=✫---

The train carrying Hamlin and Amery pulled into the station at Mainz. Both Hamlin and Amery left the station and Hamlin flagged down a taxi. A blue Mercedes pulled up next to Hamlin.

'Bring mich bitter zu den Jupitersäulen,' Hamlin said to the driver after they had both got into the car.

The driver nodded.

Amery fastened their seat belt before leaning over to Hamlin, 'Where are we going?' 'I asked him to take us to the Jupiter monument. There's something there I need to check first.'

The short drive to the monument was taken in silence. When they arrived Hamlin handed the driver a fifty Euro note.'

'Stimmt so, danke,' said Hamlin.

'Danke,' said the driver.

'You over paid him,' said Amery as they both headed to what passed for a tourist centre office.

Hamlin just nodded. He headed over to the closed office looking for opening times. 'This place should be open now. Ah, there's a note that it's closed due to "unforeseen circumstances". Well, that won't do. I need to get in there.'

Hamlin then started looking at the padlocked gate, looked at the padlock itself, smiled, and then fished a small black leather wallet from on inside pocket. He opened it and pulled out two metal rods that he inserted into the lock. A couple of seconds later the lock was opened.

'Handy skill,' said Amery.

Hamlin just replied with a knowing smile. He then had a furtive look around to ensure there was no one looking, and then slipped inside. Amery quickly followed.

Inside there was a "do not enter" style tape that the police would have put in place. This was all around the monument. They both ignored it and crossed to the monument itself.

'This is where-' started Amery.

Hamlin had gone quiet, concentration lined his face. He was looking hard at the monument, at one particular image carved into the stone. 'I helped to restore this part. Took the better part of a month. The day after we finished, Freyja was born. Her mother was from Norway, and her grandmother mother was called Freyja too. She loved her grandmother so much that there was no real choice on the name.' Hamlin smiled at the memory.

The smile was short lived.

Next to the monument was the sheet with the Latin writing on it. It looked like a bed sheet. Hamlin knelt next to the sheet to hold it in his hands. He picked up a corner and gently rubbed it, 'Not silk, but expensive.'

He stopped rubbing as his fingers found a monogram. A stylised F and G combined.

Amery could see the alarm in Hamlin's face, 'What is it?'

'Georg. But he died ten years ago,' Hamlin said.

Campfires, Bonfires and Gun Fire

Hamlin was examining the remains of a fire around the base of the monument. The lower third of the pillar was blackened with soot from the flames. This wasn't an attempt at sacrifice or part of any ritual that Hamlin was aware of associated with any aspect of ancient Roman religion.

This was an attempt to destroy the monument itself.

The charred earth around it spread for a metre in each direction there was ash and charcoal in in the dark circle. Hamlin couldn't tell if there was any organic material, or to be precise, any human remains, within the detritus, but he didn't think there was.

'Someone doesn't like this monument,' said Amery.

'I'm concerned that it may be someone who should not actually be alive,' replied Hamlin.

'Officially, that includes you.' Amery knelt besides Hamlin and started to rake their fingers through the ashes, not really sure what they hoped to find.

Hamlin chuckled softly at the comment and nodded. 'I think I need to call Hallus, but he'll be in the air soon if he is not already so we will have to wait until the morning.'

After Hamlin had taken a few photos of the scene on his phone, they both left through the gate. Hamlin carefully locked the padlock once more. 'No one will even know we were here,' he said.

---☆=☆---

Amery woke with a start.

They'd found a cheap hotel near to the monument that had two rooms vacant; Hamlin paid for both. Speaking fluent German, Hamlin convinced the receptionist that he was James Meyer, along with a suitable passport, from Berlin and he was Amery's long-lost father from an estranged marriage. The receptionist was not buying it until Hamlin had asked for two rooms. Amery's room was three doors down from Hamlin's, but at least they were both on the same floor.

The noise, Amery realised, that had roused them from sleep was coming from the TV at the far end of the room. With so much going on in the last few days, Amery was finding it difficult to find sleep, so they'd put on the TV and found the only English speaking channel the hotel had for free, BBC World Service.

Exhaustion was the only reason they had fallen asleep.

The programme on TV was news of a war in some Eastern European country some years ago and how the way current politics were brewing meant the war could return. The noise that had woken Amery was of a riot and looting; the authorities had got involved to quell the rioters. Amery muted the TV after even the news anchor and the roving reporter didn't agree on the pronunciation of the town where the fighting had started.

Amery turned off the TV after a few more minutes of watching, politics was a pet peeve and something they avoided as much as possible. Their opinion of war was the physical manifestation of conflicting politics, and something to be avoided even more.

Sitting up in bed, knees tucked under their clasped arms, Amery considered the absurdity of the situation they found themselves within.

A few days ago, life was normal. They were looking forward to a new job, but now they may actually be the grandchild of an immortal Roman slave, and their own life may be extended longer than should be natural.

There was a knock on the door. 'Amery, it's me.'

Amery got up after another knock, 'Alright. I'm up' They grabbed the complimentary robe from the hotel and put it on as they walked over to the door.

When Amery opened the door, Hamlin walked straight in without being asked. 'Good morning?' Amery said. After looking at their watch they saw it was 4am; darkness still dominated the world outside Amery's hotel window.

'I've just spoken to Hallus, he landed in Manchester over an hour ago. His man says your mum is OK and he is going to meet with them all. Apparently, she's wild camping with her friend Sarah?'

'Yeah, they do that a lot. Since she retired, she goes for a couple of weeks every now and then.'

'I've also been looking up the things I saw at the Jupiter monument. I think whoever this is was actually trying to destroy it. There is a rumour that the one in Mainz is the oldest. It isn't, it is also a made up of replica parts and not completely original.

'I can't see why they would want to do this, but I have my suspicions.' Hamlin sat down heavily on the bed.

Amery pulled up a chair. 'Spill Prof. You have that "I know what is going on, but don't want to say" look. You do that a lot.'

Hamlin rubbed his eyes, stood up and walked to the window. 'I think this is Georg. I think he is trying to bring an end to my, and Hallus', extended life. I am not sure why though, yet.'

Out of the window, Hamlin could see a car with two people in the front. He pointed at them and beckoned Amery over, 'I also think that these two have been following us since the train station.'

Amery cautiously looked through the window and saw the car Hamlin was referring to.

'I think we need to have a quiet word with them. Leave your light on, and keep wandering by the window every now and then. I will pop down there and introduce myself,' said Hamlin.

'Be careful,' said Amery.

Hamlin set off for the lift whilst Amery changed clothes. If they were up, may as well get dressed they thought.

Outside the hotel Hamlin stayed in the shadows and wandered down the street away from the car. Once he was sure he was out of sight he crossed over and doubled back. It was difficult to stay hidden, with all the streetlights and passing cars, but Hamlin had many years of training. He could have disappeared in front of someone looking at him, if he tried hard enough.

When he reached the car, there was a problem. The path to the car was under the glare of a streetlight, there was no getting around this. Hamlin would need a distraction, so he called Amery.

'Are you ready?' he said when Amery answered.

'I'm dressed and packed. Yep. What do you have in mind?' Amery said.

'Turn out the lights, and leave the room. Don't check-out though, just head for the stairs.'

As soon as Amery turned out the light, the two men in the car reacted. The driver nudged his companion who was reading something. He pointed to the window for Amery's room and then they both started to leave the car.

Hamlin reacted immediately.

From the darkness of his hiding place, Hamlin rushed to the car and heavily shut the door on the driver's leg. The driver howled in pain as door smacked into his shin bone. His surprised partner ran round the car fumbling at a gun from inside his jacket. Before he could fire, Hamlin swung the driver's door into the running man's path. The man managed to fire a shot, but his aim was deflected by the door hitting him.

The bullet hit the streetlight and the light went out.

Amery ran to the door when they heard the gun shot, fearing that Hamlin had been hurt. They saw Hamlin kick the stomach of man holding the gun, who then doubled over and dropped the firearm.

Hamlin picked up the gun and stripped it back to its parts in a heartbeat. He tossed the mag into a nearby litter bin.

'Who are you? And what do you want?' Amery heard Hamlin say in German. 'Why are you following us?'

The man on the floor, breathing heavily, crawled into the light of the streetlight. It was Marcus Durand. In French he said, 'We're French police.'

'A little out of your jurisdiction, are you not?' said Hamlin in French.

'I am Marcus Durand,' said the man on the floor.

'I recognise you,' said Hamlin in English. 'You work for Delisle. Why are you following me?'

'The inspector,' coughed Durand, 'wanted me to track you down, Monsieur Stafford. Or is it Herr Meyer?'

Lambert howled again in pain.

Hamlin opened the door, gently this time, and looked at the man's leg. 'You'll live. You'll have a bruise for a while, but nothing is broken so stop crying like a baby.'

'What's going on?' Amery had joined them.

'French police,' said Hamlin.

Amery was confused.

'I apologise,' said Durand as he stood. 'We were meant to be observing. We tracked you to the train station based on similar reports of the murder at the Jupiter monument. You went by train, we flew to Frankfurt airport directly, about thirty minutes from here. Thankfully we arrived at the station about twenty minutes before you did.'

'So you saw us break into the monument?' asked Amery.

'We did,' grunted Lambert. He was furiously rubbing his shin.

'But we wanted to see what you were doing before we acted,' said Durand.

'Why were you leaving the car when Amery turned out the light?' said Hamlin.

'Well, the light had been on all night so we were concerned something bad had happened. We were coming to make sure you were safe,' Durand gestured towards Amery.

'Thank you, but I am quite well.'

---✶=✶---

Hallus arrived at the location Aaron had given him, but all he found was a ruined tent. The smoke from the flames tearing away at the tent fabric was visible for miles. Even in the dark.

The charred hand poking out from the side looked male. Hallus was running over now. He kicked at the burning tent to clear it away from the body of the man, clearly it was Aaron.

The boots looked familiar.

Next to the tent, scratched into the earth were the words: "Malum, mecum Herculem ad Columnam"

'Meet me at the Pillar of Hercules?'

Consequences

allus looked about and found the belongings of Harriet, Amery's mother. She was nowhere to be found. After a little more searching, Hallus found a dark-haired woman's body near the campsite, or at least most of her.

He was saddened by the woman's death, and by that of Aaron's. Aaron had worked for Hallus since he was a teenager, that was nearly twenty years ago now. He would have to inform Aaron's family; a job he had grown to detest over the many years of his life.

So many people he had known, and loved, had passed on into the afterlife and he longed to see a large number of them again. At least one day. He knew they were all at peace, and that brought him some peace too, but he hated how death took everyone. He was thankful he had Hamlin.

He fished out his phone, it would be 6am in Germany right now, but he needed to speak to his friend.

The phone was answered almost immediately.

'You're up already?' said Hallus.

'Yeah, trouble with some gendarmes,' replied Hamlin.

'In Germany? No, don't explain. No time. Just listen.' Hallus then explained that Harriet was missing, likely taken by whoever was doing all this and now on the way to the Pillar of Hercules. Gibraltar.

'Why is it always Gibraltar?' asked Hamlin. 'OK, we'll get there as fast as we can.'

--- ✭ = ✭ ---

'This freak has my Mum? I'll rip his lungs out.' Amery was incensed. They'd been like that the whole time they sat in the departures lounge at Frankfurt airport. Over an hour now since Hamlin and Amery had arrived.

'Right now, I can't see that your mum will be harmed. This guy is after me and Hallus. Your mum is just a piece in his game,' said Hamlin.

The announcement over the tannoy said that their plane was ready for boarding, so they both headed for their gate.

Durand and a limping Lambert had come to the airport too, they were heading back to Paris. Their flight was not for a few hours but the two detectives joined Hamlin and Amery in waiting. Now the flight to Gibraltar was boarding, Durand stepped up to shake Hamlin's hand.

'Despite the bruising to my pride,' Durand said in French, 'I think letting you go is right. I can't stop you anyway.'

'What will you go tell your inspector?' asked Amery in English.

'We couldn't stop you leaving for another country,' replied Lambert. 'What else but the truth?' He shrugged.

'We can't follow to Gibraltar, it is outside the EU after all now. So this is where we must part. For now,' said Durand.

Hamlin smiled and headed for the gate, closely following Amery who had already handed their boarding pass to the man waiting by the gate. He handed his boarding pass over right after, the flight attendant scanned the bar code and then handed it back. 'Safe flight,' said the man with a practiced smile.

---☆=☆---

Their flight to Gibraltar was uneventful, however, the landing at the tiny airport was quite an event for Hamlin. He had never flown to Gibraltar before; he considered it a second home. At passport control, he pulled out the James Hamlin passport.

After they were through, Amery asked why he'd used that one.

'I have apartments here. Officially I am from here as far as my passport says,' he said. His accent had changed too. He now even spoke with a Gibraltarian twang.

Amery chuckled. 'Where are we meeting Hallus?'

'He lands in,' Hamlin checked his watch, 'roughly five hours. So we will meet him at our favourite bar for a meal.'

'We're not here for the tourism,' spat Amery.

'The Star Inn is the oldest bar in Gibraltar, there is a secret room in there that even the owner does not know about. But there are "supplies" we can use in there. Hence why we are meeting there. A "meal" is not what you're thinking,' Hamlin tapped his nose and wore a knowing smile. 'OK, now we're talking.'

---✶=✶---

Hallus was at Gatwick airport looking for the right check-in desk for his flight when a gruff voice whispered in his ear, 'If you get on that plane, your daughter will be spread all over Europe in small bags.'

Hallus made an attempt to turn his head.

'Look at me and-' said the man's voice. A hard prod in Hallus' back told him that the man was armed.

'Yeah I get it. I've been told to go though,' Hallus said.

'No. Not you. Not yet. Give me your phone.'

Hallus fished out his phone and handed it over his shoulder. A rough hand took it and crushed it next to

Hallus's left ear. Tiny shards of glass and plastic pinged against his ear and cheek.

'Three days,' said the man.

'Three days for what?' said Hallus.

There was no reply.

'Oh, giving it the strong silent treatment, eh?'

A few seconds later Hallus realised the man had gone. He slowly turned to see there was no one around that could have been standing next to him. There were lots of people milling about, many joining snaking lines to various check-in desks. Some heading over to departure gates, a few airport staff, but no one that looked out of place.

Having not checked in or passed through security, Hallus left the airport. Without Aaron by his side, a constant companion for many years, he felt exposed. Outside the airport he headed for the taxi rank and climbed into a waiting black cab.

'Windsor please,' he told the driver.

'Sure,' replied the driver.

When the cab was moving, Hallus reached into his shoe and pulled out an old-style mobile. No smart touch screen, just functional numbers and a small single line for the number or text. He typed out a message to Hamlin: "Problem. Been told to stay away by person unknown. Be there soon."

The Choice

2 8 BCE. Mons Calpe (Gibraltar) ... Hallus was laying on the floor as kick after kick swung in to his gut. His hands were over his head to protect his face as the three men beat him within an inch of his life.

'You are my property!' screamed Garallius Gabinus between the three men attacking Hallus. Spittle showered from his mouth over Hallus' arms and what little was exposed of his face.

A moment later, Garallius shooed away the three men he had employed for this task. They went to stand a few feet away.

'Give us our coin, or we take it out on you too,' said the tallest of the thugs.

'Very well,' Garallius said as he fumbled for a coin pouch. He jingled it in his hand a moment before tossing it to them.

The tall man caught it and smiled. 'Nice doing business with you,' he said. The three thugs then left.

Garallius knelt down besides the heavily breathing Hallus. He brushed away a strand of hair away from Hallus' bruised and bloodied face in almost loving way. 'I never wanted this, my sweet Hallus. You are mine, you always have been. But you have disgraced my family honour, and defaced this tattoo on your arm to cover over my family crest.' Garallius rubbed a hand over the tattoo on Hallus' right forearm.

Hallus spat some blood from his mouth as he coughed.

'You take care now, my sweet. I will be seeing you soon, once I have restored my honour with that snake Hadriana. I will take from him everything. Like he took from me. And then you will return to me,' Garallius said.

Garallius held Hallus' face for a moment. Blood from Hallus' broken nose ran into the crevice where hand met face, catching a small cut on Garallius' palm. In disgust, the ex-senator quickly wiped his hand on the rags that covered Hallus' shoulder, cleaning off the blood.

---✮=✮---

Present Day... Deflated, Hamlin sagged into his chair at the Star Inn.

'What?' said Amery.

'There is an issue. Someone has warned Hallus away from taking his flight from Gatwick. Upon pain of death of your mother, apparently. He is making other arrangements to get here as soon as he can.'

Amery shot an angry look at Hamlin. 'What have you got me into?'

As they sat there the waitress came over with their drinks, and a note. She handed the note to Amery, and the bill for the two coffees to Hamlin.

On the bill, there was a scrawled "help me". Hamlin calmly thanked the shaking girl and said he would be over with the money in a moment.

She smiled thinly and departed.

Amery had gone white.

'Tell me,' said Hamlin.

Amery handed the note over, 'If I am to see my mum again, I am to stay here. You need to go up the Rock.'

Hamlin read the hand-written note. The penmanship was strangely familiar.

'Okay,' he said finally, 'let's do it this way. Go and see my friend Franz, I'll give you the address. He will help you to "disappear". I need you to meet me at the top.' He jabbed a thumb over his shoulder at the summit of the Rock of Gibraltar.

'He'll probably tell you I'm dead. He would like to think so, because he owes me a few favours. Tell him that you need the help of Jupiter, and he will know what you mean. I need to go and help this poor girl in here. She's scared of someone and I hate to let anyone feel like they are helpless,' he nodded at the waitress as she nervously dropped an empty cup on the floor.

'I thought she looked off,' said Amery.

'I will head off then to the top,' said Hamlin. 'Apparently this joker is a one for theatrics. The note says I need to wear my old senatorial robes, and I need to go by foot. That is fine, I can manage that.

'Be at the top in approximately four hours. I will take my time. Hopefully Hallus will be here by then too,' Hamlin concluded.

They both nodded. Amery stood and then hugged Hamlin. He slipped a note into Amery's pocket; the address of Franz.

'Be careful,' Amery said.

Hamlin watched Amery head off down the street and he also saw them reach for the note with Franz's address. They read it, and then scrunched it and put it back into the same pocket.

Inside the bar, Hamlin saw the waitress fumble with the cash till. He stood and wandered in with money in his hand. 'How much do I owe you?' he said pretending not to have had the bill already.

The waitress jumped and hit a button on the cash till. A new copy of the bill was printed and she nervously handed it over to Hamlin.

'Ah yes,' he handed over too much money. 'Keep the change. Any recommendations for entertainment round here?'

'Just over there,' she replied and nodded at the only other patron in the bar. It was a man sat in the shadow of a booth away from the cash till itself.

Hamlin went over and sat down opposite the man.

'Do you I know you?' said the man.

'I think you do. And I think you know what I am capable of. If you know anything about me, you will leave. Now. You will not be coming back. Ever. If I see you again I will be the last thing you ever see,' Hamlin whispered.

The man took a drink. 'Just get to the top. That is all I was supposed to say.'

The man then stood up, threw a handful of money onto the table and left.

Hamlin then went to the waitress, 'He won't be back. How did you know I could help?'

'I saw you with your friend. You looked kind,' she said.

---☆=☆---

Amery followed the map on an app on their phone, the address Hamlin had given them was at the edge of the city.

It was a rundown little house, barely even noticeable if it were not somewhere they were looking for. Amery knocked on the faded yellow door and waited.

Two minutes passed, Amery thought it rude to knock again too soon, but was about to knock when the door swung open.

'Yes?' said a tall, bearded man. The bushy ginger beard almost obscured the man's mouth.

'We have a mutual friend, James Hamlin,' said Amery.

'He's dead!' barked the man.

'You're Franz? He said I need to tell you I need the help of Jupiter.' Amery tried to make sure their face held no emotions.

'Inside. And be quick,' said Franz. He gave a furtive look up and down the street before stepping inside after Amery and then closing the door.

'What has the old goat done now?' said Franz.

'Someone is killing his family, and they have my mother. I think they are going to kill her too. But Hamlin is going to meet them at the top of The Rock,' Amery explained quickly. 'He said you could get me there too without being seen.

'Aye, I can do that. Hamlin saved my life more times than I care to mention, so I owe him. Whatever he needs, I can do. When do we need to be there?'

Amery explained that Hamlin was going to walk to the top, taking his time. They also mentioned the senatorial robes, which Franz snorted at.

'He ain't wore that in decades,' said Franz. 'He'll look like a loon going up on foot in that get up.'

'How do we get up there?' asked Amery.

'I have my ways.'

---✭=✭---

Hallus was getting into a grey Lamborghini. There was a parcel delivery locker two hundred yards away where he had retrieved the keys. The delivery drivers from the company had never understood why the bottom left locker, the smallest of the lockers, was never in use. This was where Hallus had added his own to the system.

It blended in perfectly, but was not part of the original build and was just ignored by all users; company workers and civilians alike.

In the fast car, Hallus drove to a private air strip he knew of. At the air strip he spoke to the owners and chartered a flight to Spain so that he could get as close as possible, and then cross the border into Gibraltar.

As payment for the trip, he handed the manager of the air strip the keys to the Lamborghini.

The surprised man just asked when the fool before him wanted to fly.

'Now,' was the only reply Hallus had.

---✮=✮---

28 BCE Mons Calpe ... Garallius stumbled into a cart that was being pulled along by a slave woman, 'Careful where you are going, wretch. I will have your master string you up for such carelessness.'

'Are you feeling well, sir?' said a man following the cart.

'Perfectly,' said Garallius just a moment before he vomited onto the man's feet.

'You're a drunk. Get back to the drinking house, you foul excuse for a man!' The man whipped the woman pulling his cart and they both hurried away from Garallius.

---✮=✮---

Present Day ... Hamlin went upstairs in the Star Inn. In a back room there was an odd brick set in the wall. He pulled it out and reached into the hole. There was a lever he found, pulled on and then stepped back.

The wall section before him moved inwards and slid to the left. Behind the wall was a chest that a pirate of old would have been proud of. Hamlin knocked on various locations of the chest in a certain pattern.

The lock snicked open when he finished his knocking and rapping.

Hamlin lifted the lid and air hissed out from inside. There was a pristine white toga inside the chest that Hamlin picked up.

---☆=☆---

28 BCE Mons Calpe ... Garallius Gabinus sat on the floor of the summit of the Pillar of Hercules.

It had been almost a week since he had seen Hallus, and he realised that he was neither tired nor really actually hungry. He'd not slept in three days, but he didn't feel like he needed sleep. He thought he never would ever again.

The sensations running through him since the meeting with his slave were indescribable. He felt more alive than he had ever felt.

---☆=☆---

Present Day ... Hamlin walked through the streets of Gibraltar. There were cat-callers and wolf-whistlers along every street, but he felt not one pang of embarrassment. He was a senator of Rome, and he strutted along with the feeling that this may be one of the most important days ever for him.

---☆=☆---

Hallus was sitting in the passenger seat of the small jet, they were around an hour away from landing in Spain and he was planning how he would get to The Rock.

He had sent a message to Hamlin to say that he would be arriving in a couple of hours, but he wasn't sure if his message was received. The phone in his pocket, ancient by smart phone standards, didn't have a way of confirming if the recipient had received any message.

--- ✮ = ✮ ---

Amery and Franz were making their way through several underground tunnels.

Franz had said these were constructed by cavemen before the Roman Empire was even a twinkle in the eye of "Emperor Smartypants", and then smugglers used to use them to bring goods in from the docks without the dock authorities being able to tax them, or possibly steal the good for themselves.

'We'll get to the base of The Rock soon, then we need to go outside for a spell. As long as no one is looking at us though, we won't be seen while we get to the next set of tunnels.

Race to the Top

Hamlin walked slowly, with pride. There were some jeers, some cheers and lots of laughter as he walked. Some tourists even thought he was a street performer and stopped him for photos; or tried to. He didn't stop, which caused more than a crossed word or two.

He carried on regardless. Eventually he reached the beginning of he rise to the summit, the route split at a casino. The road he took was very steep, and he knew that he had to take his time even if the road itself didn't impose that already on him.

He therefore slowed down a little.

---☆=☆---

Hallus climbed into a taxi, 'Gibraltar border crossing, please. Fast as you can. There's an extra two hundred in it for you if you can do it within two hours.' He spoke in Spanish.

The driver nodded and then shot off at alarming speed. He weaved through traffic, eliciting many angry reactions from other drivers.

The private air strip his charter plane had landed at was just over an hour and a half away from the border in good traffic. This wasn't good traffic.

Hallus pulled out his phone and dialled Hamlin's number. Again. As the last few times he had tried, the call was unanswered. After four rings the now familiar "This is me. Leave a message after the beep. You know how this works" recorded response played. 'By Jupiter! Answer your damned phone, old man,' he sighed.

He had picked up Harriet's phone from the campsite and he hoped he could turn it on and use it. Thankfully, the phone started up.

Unfortunately it was locked with a PIN.

Another sigh.

He put the phone in his pocket.

---✭=✭---

Amery and Franz had come to the end of the smuggler tunnels, and had to go out into the open.

Franz went first. He casually looked around, let the warm, late afternoon breeze brush against him. There were some tourists, three women and a man, sat on a low wall nearby. They'd not spotted Franz, they were deep in conversation talking about the strange man they'd just seen in a Roman style toga, and laughing about it.

Franz smiled as he realised they were probably talking about Hamlin. He waved over to Amery hiding in the brush behind him. They came out as casually as possible.

'Nope, I can't find Gigi in there,' Amery said. One of the women on the wall had spotted Amery clamber through the wild hedgerow.

Franz looked confused for a moment before realisation dawned. 'I'm sure we'll find your, er, puppy soon,' he said.

The woman didn't bat an eyelid and returned to the conversation with her friends.

'Over there,' Franz said quietly and pointed across the road.

Amery followed him down a side street, away from the very steep road that led up the hill. They assumed that was where Hamlin had gone, 'Isn't that the way we need to go?'

'Not if you don't want to be seen,' said Franz.

---★=★---

25 CE, Rome...Garallius stood at the edges of the cemetery. His family had long since shunned him as a disciple of Orcus, a god of the underworld.

His daughter had accused Garallius of striking a deal with Orcus to unnaturally extend his own life. Garallius had denied it, but he could not defend that claim. He was chased away with people throwing stones and threatening him with swords and knives.

Today, his daughter's family, her two sons, were laying her to test in the family tomb of her husband. She'd turned sixty three only four days before, a significant age. Her husband had died many years before on the frontier of the empire.

Garallius could only watch from a distance.

---✶=✶---

Present Day...The phone in Hallus' pocket, Harriet's, began to ring. Hallus answered.

'My sweet Hallus,' said the sickly sweet voice of Garallius, 'how nice it is to speak to you once more.'

'Dominus?' replied Hallus. Old habits resurfaced without any prompting from his old master and owner.

'Oh, how good of you to remember me,' sarcasm dripped through the phone's speaker into Hallus' ear.

'You should be-' started Hallus.

'I should be what? Dead? No, like you I've outlived even good old Methuselah. How long did he live according to the Christians? Nine hundred years? A thousand? No matter, we're here, he's not,' said Garallius.

'You need better research,' said Hallus.

'That's by the by, I'm not calling you for that. Your descendant lives, for now. For how long, who knows. Once I've disposed of that snake Hadriana, finally, we'll find out.'

'Garallius you've got the wrong man. It's me that you want,' said Hallus.

'Nice try,' Garallius said.

The call ended.

---✯=✯---

359 CE, Italy ...Garallius stood at the steps of the little town house in a small village that he had settled in when a messenger was running and shouting through the streets. News was spreading through the little town about "the end".

After pandemics, economic crises, recognition of Christianity, incompetent emperor after incompetent emperor, civil war, and a host of other factors, the news was no surprise to Garallius.

The Roman Empire was at an end.

He stopped the messenger boy and asked where he had heard this news, but the boy only said that he heard it from a centurion that was returning from the front. The centurion was in the town square.

Garallius went to see this centurion and was shocked to see that it was Julius Hadriana. He would recognise that face for eternity.

How he hated that man.

'How is he still as young as the last time I saw him?' he said.

'I am sorry, sir, were you talking to me,' said a man passing by.

Garallius just gave the man a disparaging look.

---✶=✶---

Present Day ...Hamlin walked slowly up the hill. He'd attracted quite a following, despite trying to tell people that he was not part of a performing arts event. He even tried being overtly nasty to some, but they took it as part of some character he was playing and laughed it off.

In his pocket, Hamlin found his phone. He'd put it on silent some time ago and when he looked at the screen he saw that he'd missed several calls from Hallus. He called him right back.

'Where are you?' said Hamlin.

'I'm at customs. Just about to pass into Gibraltar,' replied Hallus.

'That was quick. What did you do, strap on a jet engine and flap your arms?' Hamlin chuckled at the image he'd generated in his head.

Hallus laughed too. It was a rare moment they were sharing.

'I am about thirty minutes before I reach the top. And I have a trail of people following me, it's ridiculous. These people are going to get hurt if Georg has anything to say about it,' said Hamlin.

'It's not Georg. It's good old Senator Garallius Gabinus.'

'How?' said Hamlin.

'Right now, I do not know, but do not go up that hill without backup.'

Hamlin stopped.

'You still there?' said Hallus.

'I am. I've got a plan. Franz is taking Amery to the summit by the old tunnels,' said Hamlin.

'Franz? You sure? Okay, but let's hope you're not fishing him out of yet another hole. I'm through customs now, and I will get a fast ride up the hill. Be safe.' Hallus hung up.

Hamlin turned around to see around thirty people lining up behind him.

'Listen, you don't believe me, but I am going up here, probably to my death. There is a man up the top that has a gun that he will more than likely use on me. Several times. Please. I implore you. This is not an act. This is not a joke. Leave!' Hamlin screamed so loud that several of the people took a couple of paces away.

'Jeez, man! We're only having fun,' said one man.

A few more mutterings and the crowd dispersed. Apart from two.

Hamlin was about to scream again, when he saw it was Franz and Amery.

'You're going up there to die?' said Amery

'It is that senator I told you about,' said Hamlin. All the anger drained from him in a single breath out.

'There are more of you, senor?' said Franz.

'Just one, old friend. I don't know how, but I think this is all about revenge.'

Amery ran up and hugged Hamlin, 'I don't want you to die.'

Hamlin hugged Amery back. 'I will certainly try not to die. Now, go and get safe. I still need you at the top. You will need to get your Mum away from this crazy fool.

---✮=✮---

1956 CE, Vienna, Austria ...Garallius stood in Rathaus-platz, the Vienna City Hall stood behind him. Proudly in his hands was a Geburtsurkunde, a birth certificate for Georg Huber and a smile crossed his face.

He had put the final stages of his plan in motion. "Georg" was born and in roughly twenty years, maybe slightly more, he would track down his nemesis and make him pay. Somehow.

Now it was time to build a history for Georg, to show that this person really does exist.

---✮=✮---

Present Day ...Hallus was in a tourist van heading for the summit of the rock. He was praying to Jupiter that he arrived in time and could save his friend.

Amery and Franz were approaching the end of the tunnels that Franz was taking them through. Early twilight was beginning to filter through the cave and tunnel network. Their flash lights were leading the way so that they didn't get lost.

Hamlin was nearly at the top. His makeshift entourage had long dispersed. He rounded a corner in the road and saw the summit was a few hundred yards away. Near the edge, Hamlin could see a lone figure.

Finis

Hamlin slowly walked towards the shadowy figure. He could see a dull metal thing glinting off the early moonlight in his right hand.

Hamlin thought it must be a gun. 'Shooting me won't help, Senator. I've been shot many times, more than I can recall. Stabbed too. I always seem to recover.'

'I'm not going to shoot you, you fool. This is for her,' Garallius gestured over to a huddled figure who moaned at the thought of being shot.

'Why are you doing this?' Hamlin said as he circled to the left so he could take the focus away from the terrified Harriet. Hamlin recognised her now the clouds above had cleared a little and the moon shone a little brighter.

'You did this. You took everything away from me, so I am going to do the same to you. And then you will have nothing. For eternity. Just like me,' shouted Garallius.

'I did what? You offended my house. Roman law allowed me to take what I wanted of yours in compensation. Hallus was that compensation. You treated him so badly, even for a slave,' Hamlin said as he moved further to the left.

'Stand still!' Garallius sceamed.

There was a sound to the right, a small stone rattled down a wall.

'Who's there? Show yourself!' said Garallius. His voice cracked a little as he spoke, nervous energy was gripping tight over him.

A barbary ape loped out of the shadows, leered at Garallius and then sat down.

'Shoo, you stinking monkey!' shouted Garallius.

Hallus arrived at the top and saw the scene. He could see Garallius and Hamlin prowling like wounded lions around each other. On the floor he could see someone bound and gagged, sobbing. He assumed that was his daughter, Harriet, but he could not see her face.

He kept low to the ground and started creeping in the shadows to the right, just out of sight of the ape that was the focus of attention. He picked up another rock and threw it behind Garallius.

It had the desired effect.

Garralius immediately turned and fired a shot.

Hamlin, a little startled by the gun's retort, saw that the pistol was an old dull silver revolver, carrying six shots when full. Now there were five.

Hallus made a whistling noise like a night-bird, which Hamlin immediately recognised as something He and Hallus started to use in their days with Captain Columbus.

---✯=✯---

1494, Guadeloupe, Lesser Antilles ...Night had fallen and the captain, Christopher Columbus, had given his men leave to go ashore and take some time for themselves.

Hallus was not one for partying like the majority of the ship's company, however. He had other ideas. He'd seen a strange tree that bore a hard, hairy fruit. He was intrigued, and more than a little full of rum, and so he had set off on a coconut hunt.

His long-time friend and confident, James Stafford, saw him leave the camp and headed out to look after his drunken friend.

Hallus saw a tree with a large number of coconuts hanging from the top, but he didn't see the shrine some of the locals had placed at the foot of the tree. In a drunken haze, Hallus clambered through the shrine to the foot of the tree.

A native saw the transgression and immediately took offence. He grabbed a horn and blew it, the sound would have alerted others had Hamlin not interceded. He threw a fallen coconut into the brush near the native man. The noise of his horn stopped immediately and the man started to look about for whatever had made the movement.

Hamlin then made a whistle, like a Robin. This awoke a self-preservation sense in Hallus who then turned and ran away from the native.

The native didn't follow.

---✮=✮---

Present Day ...Hamlin knew the whistle. It was the American Robin, the noise that both he and Hallus had used as an alert system for each other for many, many years.

'Your friends can't save you. I am sure you must know this, Senator,' said Garallius.

'We've neither of us been privileged to use that title for far too long,' Hamlin said. His eyes were scanning the darkness to try and locate Hallus. He was glad his friend was here.

Amery and Franz reached the end of the tunnels, and they too could see the bizarre scene of two Roman senators circling each other. The noise of the gunshot had alerted them to turn off their flash lights well before they reached the exit.

'Which is which?' said Amery.

'The one with no weapon is Hamlin,' aid Franz, 'he does not condone the use of them. Not since the wars of the worlds.'

Amery was about to correct Franz, but thought better to leave him to it.

From the cave entrance, Amery could see their mother. They could see she was tied up near to the edge of the cliff. Amery could see that she was terrified and was huddling against the rock for fear of falling down the cliff onto the beach that was so far below them right now it was scary to think about. No one would be able to survive such a fall.

Amery had also heard the whistle. 'That is not a native bird to these regions,' they said. 'That has got to be Hallus.'

'How do you know?' asked Franz.

'Oh, you go camping enough and you get to know these things stuck out in the wilds and no internet. My mum got me into amateur bird watching as a kid.'

'Keep your friends close, but your enemies closer. So they say Julius,' Garallius had said. Amery had lost track of the conversation between Hamlin and the crazy man with the gun.

'More like keep your friends close but make sure to keep the ones who know your deepest, darkest, blackest secrets close so that when they no longer serve your goals you can push them off a cliff.' Hamlin looked down over the edge. The beach below was a long way down.

'I like that,' Garallius said.

This was a man who Hamlin had once admired. He was a shining light in the Senate House, someone to model your career on as an upcoming politician. The way the man treated others though, Hamlin had learned, made him rethink his admirations.

Garallius was smiling wistfully. 'And if the fall doesn't kill you, maybe this will.' He twisted his wrist a little to re-iterate that he was holding the gun.

'Please, stop this now!' Hamlin said. His eyes were transfixed on the pistol

'Not sure why I should. I was betrayed, by you, by the Senate and by my own daughter, Julius. I don't take that well. From there it's a slippery slope to all sorts of mischief.' Garallius pulled back the hammer on the revolver.

'Betrayed you?'

'Yes.' Garallius motioned with the revolver that Hamlin should continue walking, right off the cliff edge. 'Even you could not survive a fall of this height.'

Hamlin was inches away now from certain death, the heel of his left shoe just caught the edge and caused a small flurry of stones and dirt to begin crumbling down the cliff face. 'I did not cause this. But if you put the gun down, if you let Harriet go, then maybe we can work through the issues.'

It was clear Hamlin was stalling for time.

There was another whistle. This time off behind Garallius. Hamlin smiled.

'What are you smiling at, snake?' Said Garallius.

'You're not going to win this day,' said Hamlin.

'Oh, but I already have,' replied Garallius. 'Your dear friend, my sweet Hallus, is not going to be able to save you this time. Or your other brat, that Amery. Once I have disposed of your daughter here, then I will get rid of them too. You'll just be a loose end and once you've been tied off,' he smiled at his gallows humour, 'I'll be home free. Free to enjoy eternity without seeing your sad face once again. Oh, and then I will take Hallus back as a slave and put him back into his rightful place, under my heel!' He laughed.

Hamlin made a step towards Garallius at the mention of Hallus. The flash of light on the pistol made him think again. 'You have your information all wrong. Please, let's talk,' said Hamlin.

Hamlin was not worried about being shot himself, but he could not see others being hurt. Especially innocents. It was true that a bullet was a minor inconvenience at worst to Hamlin, but they still hurt when they hit. A lot. And the healing process usually took weeks. However, get a normally fatal injury in one or two specific areas and there was no knowing what would happen.

'Don't be silly Julius, you should know that I look after this very well.'

'Okay, lets get some things straight,' sighed Hamlin. 'Firstly, I have not been known as Julius Hadriana for nearly two millennia. I have changed my name several times since those days.'

'I don't care what you call yourself. I am still going to shoot your daughter here,' said Garallius, 'like I did with Freyja, and Eloise and the pathetic Benard. You know he begged for his life.'

'They are not like us, our offspring,' said Hamlin.

'No. They can die.' Garallius raised the gun and pointed at Harriet.

Through the gag, Harriet screamed.

Garallius fired three shots in her direction, just as Hallus leapt into action.

The first bullet went through Harriet's thigh, just missing any major arteries.

The second bullet went wildly off course and the third bullet pierced Hallus' heart.

'No!' screamed Garallius.

The distraction was all Hamlin needed. He shot forward and grabbed Garallius' right arm, pushing his hand to point skyward.

Garallius could not point the gun down and he fired another two shots, emptying the revolver.

Hamlin swung a fist at Garallius' chin, a powerful haymaker. Garallius spun full circle on the spot, but he didn't fall down.

Instead, Garallius stumbled a few steps to the left, then to the right and then back to the left. Hamlin tried to catch him before he fell over the edge of the cliff, but he was too late.

Hamlin could only watch in horror as Garallius fell down the cliff face, hitting rocks and out-cropping after out-cropping as he tumbled over and over, down and down, before finally splashing into the crashing waves.

Amery had run over and was working on the bindings holding her mother down. Franz was tying a torniquet, made from the sleeve of his shirt, around Harriet's leg above the gunshot wound.

Hallus didn't move. His dead, glassy eyes stared at the sight of the distant Jupiter in the clear night sky.

Epilogue

It had been two days since the events at the top of The Rock. Hallus' body had been taken to the morgue in the central hospice in Gibraltar. He had been declared dead at the scene.

Amery's mother, Harriet had to have surgery on the wound she had received, but the doctors expected a full recovery. Amery had hardly left the hospital where Harriet was being treated.

Local Police and Interpol had questioned everyone and had determined that Georg Huber of Austria, was deranged and had somehow convinced himself that Hamlin and Hallus were immortal, and that he was some long-dead Roman Senator himself.

The testimonials of everyone, including Harriet, backed up the story that they had constructed. The prints on the revolver recovered at the scene were that of Georg Huber, and therefore no other evidence was to be taken into consideration.

No case was brought against any of them for the death of Georg, or rather Garallius. His broken body had been recovered from the rocks at the base of the cliff.

'What will you do now,' Amery asked when they were walking with Hamlin in the hospital grounds.

'Not much. I was going to take a new identity, as I always do. But I think I may stick around for a bit. There is some life left in James Hamlin yet,' Hamlin chuckled.

'Ah, my friends,' said Franz as he joined them. It is good to see you both. 'How is your mother, Amery?'

'She is doing well. The doc said she could go home at the end of the week so I have flights booked and everything.' Amery said.

'That is excellent. Well, Boss, I have sorted out the problem,' said Franz.

'Excellent. Well, better get him fixed up then. Can't have Methuselah waiting another two days, can we?' said Hamlin.

---✶=✶---

In the morgue, the coroner was about the begin the autopsy on the body recovered from the top of The Rock. He opened the door of the chilled unit and saw it was empty.

He went to the desk to check the documentation, but there was nothing there. The clipboard where he was sure he last saw the file for the deceased, that was no longer in the chiller, was gone. The clipboard was bare.